JAMESTOWN SETTLEMENT

POWHATAN
TERRITORY

JAMESTOWN

JAMES

RIVER

COASTLINE

JAMESTOWN

ATLANTIC

0   250 miles

0   1/2 mile

N
W   E
S

Disney's POCAHONTAS

A Long Way Home

by Bettina Ling

Illustrations by David McCamley, Gillian Coughlan,
Kathy Bailey and D. Blakely Fuller

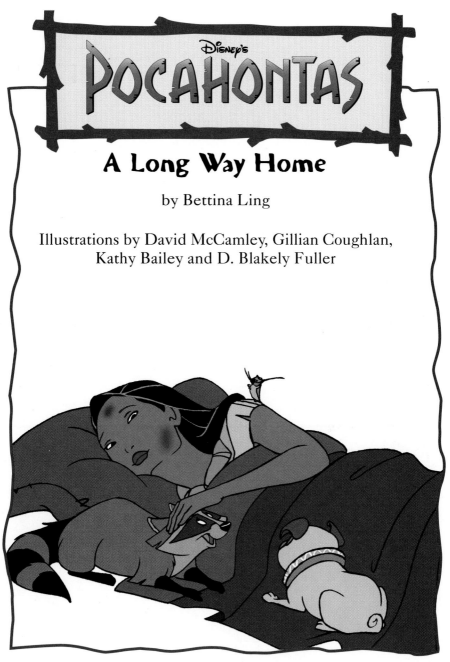

Grolier Books

Published by Grolier Books.
©1995 The Walt Disney Company. No portion of this book may be reproduced
without the consent of The Walt Disney Company.
Produced by Mega-Books, Inc.
Design and art direction by Michaelis/Carpelis Design Assoc., Inc.
Printed in the United States of America.

ISBN: 0-7172-8472-7

CHAPTER 1

Pocahontas, you're daydreaming again," said Nakoma.

Pocahontas sat under a hickory tree. Flit, her hummingbird friend, was perched on a basket next to her.

Pocahontas looked up, startled. "What, Nakoma?"

"I said, you're daydreaming again." Nakoma took Pocahontas's hands to help her up. But she changed her mind and sat down next to Pocahontas.

It was late in the autumn. Pocahontas and Nakoma were collecting nuts and wild roots. Their people, the Powhatan Indians, would store this food for the winter.

When the girls had left their village that morning, it had been cool, brisk, and clear. Now clouds were rolling in, and it was getting much colder as the wind began to pick up.

"You've been lost in thought since this morning, when we visited the fort of the English settlers," Nakoma said. "What's bothering you?"

"Oh, it's nothing really." Pocahontas sighed.

"I bet you're thinking about John Smith, aren't you?" Nakoma placed her hand on Pocahontas's shoulder.

"Nakoma, when I'm with the English settlers, they remind me of John. It's been months since he was wounded and taken back to his village of London," she said. "Even though he never said he'd come back, I can't help hoping he might return someday."

"It takes a long time to heal from a serious wound like John's," said Nakoma.

"Yes, I know. John was so brave, taking the bullet himself when that horrible man Ratcliffe tried to shoot my father," said Pocahontas.

"At least be happy with the news from the settlers that he is alive," Nakoma said.

Pocahontas smiled and nodded. "I may never see John again, but he is still in my thoughts and dreams."

"Come on, Pocahontas, let's go down into the gorge and get some chinquapins. They're your favorite nuts." The girls got up and began walking toward the gorge.

"Nakoma, I heard something this morning—" Pocahontas began, but she was interrupted by a sudden commotion under a rhododendron bush.

Out came Meeko, the mischievous raccoon who was one of Pocahontas's constant companions. Meeko had a hickory nut, stolen from Nakoma's basket, in his mouth. He was being chased by Percy, the pug dog who had belonged to Ratcliffe. When Ratcliffe was sent to prison in England, Percy had gone to live with Ratcliffe's former servant, Wiggins.

"Hey, you two, watch it!" Nakoma said as the animals chased each other around the feet of the two girls. Meeko and Percy dashed off.

Pocahontas watched the animals race away. "Sometimes when I look at Percy, it reminds me of that horrible Ratcliffe." Nakoma nodded in agreement.

"As I was saying, I overheard some disturbing news at the settlers' village. Ratcliffe—and two other men—have escaped from the prison in London." Pocahontas added in a frightened voice, "The settlers were telling everyone to be on the lookout for the three men in case they ever come back here. Ratcliffe was still talking about finding gold."

Nakoma frowned. "Gold. I thought John Smith told everyone there wasn't any of that yellow stuff around here."

"He did. But I guess Ratcliffe didn't believe him." Pocahontas shrugged her shoulders.

"The settlers gave descriptions of the two men with him. Their names are Reg and Sawbones. They're supposed to be very dangerous!" Pocahontas shivered.

The girls reached the edge of a cliff overlooking a deep gorge. Down in the gorge were beech, oak, pine, and chinquapin trees. Bushes and shrubs covered the area. A stream choked with reeds and wild grasses flowed along the bottom of the gorge.

Sheer rock walls bounded both sides of the gorge. The near wall rose to meet the cliff edge where the girls stood. At the far end of the gorge, the cliff edge overlooked layers of slate and boulders, with patches

of brush and dead grass. A rugged path wound down into the gorge among the boulders and brush.

"There are the chinquapins, near the stream," Pocahontas said. "Let's climb down."

Nakoma looked over the cliff edge. "It's too steep here, and there's not much to hang on to. Let's use that path farther down." She pointed to the far end of the gorge.

Pocahontas, always ready for a challenge, said, "It's all right. Look, there are roots growing out of the crevices between the rocks. We can hang on to those. "

"The path isn't far, and it's safer." Nakoma headed to the right. "Come on, let's go down that way."

"But it will take longer. It's getting cold, and I want to get back to the village before dark." Pocahontas was already tying the handle of her basket to the buckskin belt under her cloak. "Look, you wait here. I'll go down and get the chinquapins myself. It won't take me long."

"Pocahontas, please don't go this way. It's not safe," Nakoma pleaded.

But Pocahontas had started to climb down the rock wall. Strong and agile, she worked her way down, grabbing hold of small roots and crevices in the rock.

Halfway down, she looked up. Nakoma, Flit, Meeko, and Percy were watching her. All four looked worried.

Pocahontas laughed. "See, I'm almost at the bottom. I told you it would be all—" The rock under her hand gave way, and she lost her grip. Pocahontas grabbed for a root, but more rocks came loose. She struggled to hold on, but every movement pulled away more rock.

Then part of the cliff wall came completely away. With a scream, Pocahontas hurtled to the floor of the gorge.

CHAPTER 2

Pocahontas lay still on the forest floor. She had landed on her back, and one foot was twisted. Flit buzzed frantically above her head.

Frightened, Nakoma called down to Pocahontas, "Are you all right? Pocahontas, can you hear me?"

Pocahontas did not move. Meeko scrambled down the cliff. He jumped the last few feet to the ground.

Meeko patted Pocahontas with his paw.

He tried to wake her by licking her face and gently tugging on her hair.

Flit joined in, taking tiny strands of Pocahontas's hair in his beak and lightly pulling. She didn't move.

Percy raced back and forth at the top of the cliff, barking furiously.

"Come on, Percy, we have to get down there and help Pocahontas," Nakoma said.

She rushed along the top of the cliff to the path at the far end. Percy ran after her. At last, Nakoma and Percy reached Pocahontas, both of them out of breath from running.

From what Nakoma could see, Pocahontas had the beginnings of bruises on her face and arms and a cut on her leg. Nakoma noticed another cut as well as a bump on the side of Pocahontas's head. Nakoma inspected the twisted foot. The ankle was swelling and turning blue, but the foot did not appear to be broken.

"Pocahontas, wake up," Nakoma cried.

Reaching under Pocahontas's cloak, Nakoma untied the basket from around her waist and walked over to the stream. She gathered a few leaves from the forest floor, covered the inside of the basket, and scooped water into it. She brought it back to Pocahontas.

Nakoma took some of the wet leaves and used them like a cloth, gently wiping Pocahontas's face. Tenderly she washed the blood from the cut on Pocahontas's leg. Pocahontas groaned softly but did not wake up.

Nakoma sat back and looked at the three animals watching her. "This is awful! Pocahontas is still unconscious. She'll need to be carried back to the village. And I'm not strong enough to do it!"

Meeko took hold of Pocahontas's cloak and tugged, looking expectantly at Nakoma.

"No, Meeko, we can't drag her all the way back to the village." Nakoma was

silent for a few moments. Finally she said, "I'll go back for help."

Nakoma felt something hit her face. It was wet. She looked up at the sky, where the clouds had turned dark. "Oh, no! It's starting to rain."

Pocahontas stirred and moaned, but she didn't wake. "If I don't bring back help before the storm begins," Nakoma said, "Pocahontas might freeze."

At the sound of the word *freeze*, Meeko jumped up and began gathering leaves. He placed them gently around Pocahontas's still form.

"Good idea, Meeko." Nakoma tucked Pocahontas's cloak tightly around her. Nakoma quickly constructed a tentlike shelter over Pocahontas and covered it with branches of pine and dead leaves. "This should keep her warm enough."

Before leaving, Nakoma tried to wake Pocahontas once more. "Pocahontas," she said softly into her ear.

Pocahontas moaned again, but she did not move.

Nakoma sighed and picked up her basket. "Percy, you come with me. Meeko and Flit, you watch over Pocahontas. I'll be back as soon as I can." With Percy barking by her side, Nakoma trotted down the gorge to the path at the far end.

Flit perched protectively on Pocahontas's shoulder. Meeko lovingly patted her face, willing her to wake up.

A long while later, Pocahontas moved slightly. Meeko and Flit looked at each other. She opened her eyes for a moment, moaned, and then closed her eyes again.

CHAPTER 3

"Pocahontas." Pocahontas thought she heard her name being called from far away. There were other words, too, but she couldn't make them out. Then Pocahontas heard her name again.

She didn't want to wake up. She was so sleepy! Someone was touching her cheek. It felt good. Finally she opened her eyes. She couldn't remember where she was.

Pocahontas's vision was cloudy. She turned her head slightly. She could just make out Flit and Meeko next to her.

Beside the animals, she thought she saw a person. She blinked a few times. As her vision cleared, she recognized the face peering down at her.

John Smith was leaning over her, smiling! He held his hand up, palm facing out, and made a circle with it. "*Wing-gap-o*," he said, giving the Powhatan greeting Pocahontas had taught him. "It's about time you woke up. You had me worried."

Pocahontas stared, shocked and delighted. "John, is it really you? I can't believe it!" She tried to sit up.

"Ow!" she said, putting her hand to the side of her head.

"Hey, be careful. You have a bump there." John tenderly supported her shoulders.

He looked at her with concern in his eyes. "How do you feel? You have some nasty cuts and bruises."

"Everything hurts. My head is swimming."

She leaned back in John's arms.

"Can you tell me what happened?" John asked.

"I fell." Pocahontas pointed to the cliff. "From there. Nakoma and I were . . ." Pocahontas stopped and looked around. "Where is Nakoma? And Percy?"

"I don't know. Only Meeko and Flit were here when I found you." Meeko and Flit watched as John moved Pocahontas to make her more comfortable. "Nakoma and Percy must have gone for help."

"I guess they did," Pocahontas said. She felt pain all over her body. Her thoughts were fuzzy.

John looked up at the cliff. "You tried to climb down that rock wall?" he asked in a tone of disbelief. "Why?"

"We were looking for . . ." Pocahontas shook her head to gather her thoughts. "For chinquapin nuts, that's it. I decided to climb down to gather the nuts, and—"

John interrupted her, upset. "That was

much too dangerous, Pocahontas."

Pocahontas pulled herself up straighter and said, "I've climbed down cliffs before. I'm very capable."

"I'm sure you are, but it was still dangerous," John said more gently. "I wish you had taken another path."

"Well, now I wish I had too!" said Pocahontas ruefully. "Some rocks came loose. I lost my grip and fell." Pocahontas tried to stand. "Ow!" she cried.

Meeko sat up, ready to help, and Flit swooped over to her shoulder. Pocahontas smiled at her animal friends' concern. "My ankle is sore. I must have twisted it."

John reached around her waist and gently pulled her up. "Here, let me support you on this side. Can you put any weight on your foot?"

"A little bit, but it's starting to swell."

"Are you able to walk?" John sounded worried. "The rain is going to turn to snow. We have to get to the village quickly or we'll be caught in a blizzard."

"If you help me, I think I can walk." Pocahontas leaned against John. "If I wrapped my ankle with some flat reeds or long grasses, it would make it easier to put weight on my foot."

"There are grasses by the stream." John lowered Pocahontas to the ground and went down to the water. Meeko and Flit followed. When they returned, Meeko and John carried long, flat rush grasses, and Flit had marsh grass trailing from his beak.

Pocahontas gingerly wrapped the flat grasses around her swollen ankle. She tied some thinner grass around the bandage to hold it in place. Then, with John's help, she stood up.

"That's better. It's a little easier to walk now." She pulled her cloak around her. "It's gotten colder. You're right, we'd better get moving."

"This time, we'll take an easier path," said John.

John and Pocahontas moved slowly down the gorge. Meeko and Flit stayed close behind. The rain fell steadily down on them all.

Pocahontas glanced at John. "I still can't believe it's you! How did you get here?"

"Your father told me where to look for you and Nakoma. But it took me quite a while to find you. I don't know these woods the way you do." John laughed.

"No, I mean when did you come back to our land?" Pocahontas stopped, resting for a moment. "No one at the fort said anything about your coming."

"I arrived on my own ship this morning." They started walking again.

John grinned. "The second we landed, I went straight to your village."

Pocahontas smiled happily. Then a worried look crossed her face. "Are you fully recovered from your wound?"

John patted his stomach. "Completely.

🕊 21 🕊

And thank you for the powdered bark from Grandmother Willow. It helped my pain."

Pocahontas looked pleased.

The pair had gone about halfway to the path when Pocahontas stopped. "Listen," she said. "Do you hear voices?"

John was quiet a moment. "I don't think so."

But Meeko and Flit were looking at the brush on one side of the gorge.

Soon there were the unmistakable sounds of people talking. The voices were getting closer.

"Maybe Nakoma has come back with some people from the village to find you."

They pushed through the foliage in the direction of the voices. But as they got closer, Pocahontas recognized the sound of English, not her Powhatan language.

One of the voices sounded familiar. Pocahontas wanted to tell John to wait. Before she could speak, out of the trees stepped Ratcliffe.

CHAPTER 4

Two nasty-looking men with shovels were behind Ratcliffe. Each group stared at the other.

Finally Ratcliffe said, "Just my luck!" Over his shoulder, he said to the men behind him, "Sawbones, Reg, I'd like you to meet John Smith and Pocahontas. The two revolting people who helped send me to prison and ruined my plans."

With an evil smile, Ratcliffe aimed his musket at John. "Don't we have some unfinished business?"

Pocahontas cried out, "John!"

"It's all right. Nobody is going to hurt us," John whispered.

Meeko dived under a bush. Flit flew up to a branch.

John looked at Ratcliffe. "So, you did escape from prison." In a commanding voice, he added, "Put that gun down. You're in enough trouble as it is."

"Keep quiet. If it weren't for you, I would have found my gold. I'd have returned to England to live a life of luxury. Instead, I'm living with thugs."

"You made your own problems. You can't blame anyone else for what happened to you." John started backing up slowly. Pocahontas moved with him. She looked to the left and right, trying to find an escape route.

"Stop right there. You two aren't going anywhere." Ratcliffe tightened his grip on the musket.

John and Pocahontas stayed still. Ratcliffe kept his musket pointed at them. He moved sideways. His eyes scanned the surrounding forest. "I'm going to have to decide what to do with you two meddlers."

One of the other men stepped forward. He was tall and muscular and looked dangerous.

"Let's get rid of them. We don't want them blabbin' to the settlers that they've seen us," the man said in a menacing tone. "We've got to stay hidden until we've found some gold. Then we can sneak back to our ship."

"Let's not be too hasty, Sawbones," Ratcliffe said. "We could use them to help us dig for the gold. I'll bet Pocahontas could tell us where to look."

Pocahontas stiffened at the sound of her name. She stared back at Ratcliffe.

"There is no gold here, as you've been told before," she said in a defiant voice.

Ignoring her, Ratcliffe said to his men, "Sawbones, Reg, check around and see if you spot anyone else. Pocahontas's friends could be nearby."

Sawbones faced Ratcliffe. "Wait a minute, now. What if we run into more Indians? How are we goin' to defend ourselves? Reg and I don't have any weapons with us!"

Ratcliffe shot the man a withering look. "You have a shovel in your hand, don't you?"

Sawbones nodded and looked blank.

Ratcliffe moved closer to Sawbones and said slowly, "Well, then, you have a weapon." He smiled stiffly at Sawbones.

"But this here is for diggin'. How're we goin' to defend ourselves if we're attacked?" Sawbones asked again.

Ratcliffe screamed at him, "Hit them over the head with your shovel, you idiot! Now get out of here."

Sawbones looked angry. "I don't like

being yelled at," he said. He advanced toward Ratcliffe.

Reg rushed forward. Although he was at least a foot shorter than Sawbones, he looked equally dangerous. He had a thick, bulging chest and arm muscles that showed even through his coat.

Reg tugged at Sawbones's sleeve. "Come on, mate. I don't like bein' out in this cold and wet. I want to get inside."

Sawbones looked from Ratcliffe to Reg and back again. He shrugged, then headed into the trees with Reg behind him.

Meeko peeked out from his hiding place under the bush.

Ratcliffe turned his full attention to John and Pocahontas again. "So, what should I do? Have you both dig for my gold? Or is it time to get the two of you out of my hair for good?"

"Now, hold on, Ratcliffe. Can't we talk this over?" Pocahontas realized John was trying to buy time until they could find an opportunity to escape. "Why did you risk coming back here for gold when you know there isn't any?"

"You didn't think I believed your lies about there being no gold here, did you? I know the Indians are hiding it." Ratcliffe looked at Pocahontas.

"I plan to find some for myself," he continued. "With the help of Sawbones and Reg. To do the digging, of course."

"There's no gold. All your efforts will be for nothing," Pocahontas told him.

"We'll see," he answered.

"How'd you and your crooked friends get here from England?" John asked.

"That's none of your concern," Ratcliffe answered. "Enough! I'm cold, and this horrid rain seems to be turning to snow."

Ratcliffe aimed his musket and walked toward Pocahontas and John. "You two have caused me enough trouble. You won't be causing me any more."

CHAPTER 5

Flit took action. He swooped down and dive-bombed Ratcliffe's head. Startled, Ratcliffe dropped his musket.

John and Pocahontas slipped into the woods, Meeko close behind them.

"Stop that, you wretched little creature!" Ratcliffe shouted as he tried to shield his face from Flit's pecks. He reached for his musket, but Flit attacked him again.

Ratcliffe yelled, "Sawbones, Reg, help!

They're getting away! Stop them!"

Pocahontas and John headed for the path that led out of the gorge. With John's help, Pocahontas managed to limp along on her injured foot, but each step was painful.

Pocahontas and John heard Ratcliffe running through the brush and then shouts, as Sawbones and Reg met up with him.

"We have to get out of the gorge fast. How is your leg?" John asked.

"I'm fine. Don't worry about me," Pocahontas answered. Having John with her gave her strength.

"Let's hide over there for a minute." John pointed to a boulder. "You need to catch your breath."

They ducked behind the boulder. Meeko and Flit hid in a hollowed-out tree stump. Everyone watched silently as Ratcliffe, Sawbones, and Reg ran by.

It became quiet. Pocahontas sat back

and sighed. "Maybe they've given up," she said.

"It's too quiet," answered John. "I think Ratcliffe's up to something. Is there another way to get out of the gorge?"

Pocahontas nodded. "There is another path, but it's much farther away."

"We'll have to take our chances, then. Keep your eyes and ears open and stay on guard," John whispered. "I'm sure they're still looking for us."

The forest was covered with a thin blanket of snow now. Pocahontas, John, Meeko, and Flit moved out from behind the boulder and continued silently on. But a few minutes later, Ratcliffe, Reg, and Sawbones came crashing out from the brush.

"Get them!" yelled Ratcliffe.

Meeko leaped on Ratcliffe's leg and took a big bite.

Ratcliffe let out a scream and fell to the ground. He let go of the musket and held

his leg. "You filthy beast!" he yelled as he tried to grab Meeko.

John pushed Pocahontas behind a fallen tree. He faced Reg and Sawbones. Flit pecked Reg's arm, causing him to drop his shovel.

"John, look out!" Pocahontas cried as Sawbones swung his shovel at John.

John ducked, then punched Sawbones, sending him flying into the bushes.

As Ratcliffe rolled on the ground in pain, Meeko dragged the musket into the bushes. Then he stuffed pawfuls of dirt and dried leaves down the barrel.

Reg swung at John but missed him. Meeko ran back to Flit. They ganged up on Reg, pecking and biting.

"Yow! Ow, ow, stop it!" Reg screamed.

John punched Reg on the jaw, knocking him out.

Ratcliffe was scrambling around on the ground looking for his musket. "What did that blasted piece of fur do with my gun?"

He found it under the bush and stood up. "Ah-hah! Thought you could fool me, you wretched creature!" Ratcliffe waved the musket triumphantly. Dirt and leaves began to fly from the barrel.

"What in blazes! He's ruined my musket!" Ratcliffe looked around for Meeko. "I'll turn you into raccoon pie when I get my hands on you."

John picked up Sawbones's shovel and took Pocahontas's arm. "Let's get out of here."

They covered the last few yards to the path. It looked as if they were going to get away. But as they started up the path, Sawbones came running from the forest and tackled John.

CHAPTER 6

Struggling, John and Sawbones fell against the cliff wall. John dropped the shovel and Pocahontas grabbed it. Ratcliffe burst out of the bushes. Holding Reg's shovel, he advanced on John.

"John, catch!" Pocahontas cried.

John leapt to his feet and Pocahontas threw him the shovel. He caught it in one hand and swung at Ratcliffe, knocking him down. Meeko leaped on Ratcliffe, bit him on the nose, and hung on.

Sawbones grabbed the shovel with both hands and wrestled John for it. Flit dive-bombed Sawbones.

The snow was falling heavily. It was difficult to see anything. Ratcliffe grabbed Meeko's tail and yanked. Meeko let go of Ratcliffe's nose and slid out of his grasp.

Ratcliffe stood up and yelled at Sawbones, "Leave them. Let's find Reg and get out of here before this storm becomes a blizzard!" Holding his bloody nose, Ratcliffe disappeared into the gorge.

Sawbones managed to wrestle the shovel away from John. Sawbones turned and hit John in the leg. John yelled in pain and fell to the ground, hitting his head.

"Now see how far you'll get in this storm!" With a laugh, Sawbones was gone.

Pocahontas ran to John. He was lying still. "John, are you all right?" she cried.

John moaned.

Pocahontas looked at John's leg. His trousers were ripped. His leg was bleeding from a nasty gash. Pocahontas touched his face. "John, can you hear me?"

John moved and groaned. His eyelids fluttered open. He looked up at her. "Pocahontas?" He closed his eyes again.

"I'm here, John. Stay still. Your leg is hurt. I'm going to wrap something around the cut to stop the bleeding."

Pocahontas reached under her cloak and undid her buckskin belt. She cleaned the wound with wet snow and tied her soft belt around John's leg. John moaned. Pocahontas worked quickly, ignoring the pain from her own injuries. She still felt weak, but her concern for John pushed away all thoughts about herself.

Meeko and Flit watched from a rock.

"John, please, you have to wake up!" Pocahontas patted his face. John's eyelids opened again. This time they stayed open.

"Pocahontas, my leg—it hurts," he said, dazed.

"You have a bad cut, John. And you may have sprained your ankle when you went down. Do you think you can get up if I help you?"

"I'll try. It's hard to stay awake. I feel like my head is stuffed with cotton. Can't think straight," John mumbled. He tried to sit up but fell back.

He struggled again, and this time was able to sit up. But he was groggy. With Pocahontas's help, he stood, leaning heavily on her. Weak because of her own injuries, she had trouble supporting him. They fell against the rock wall on one side of the path. John slid to the ground.

"We need a crutch. You can lean on that, and I won't have as much of your weight on me." Pocahontas looked around.

The world had turned white. She looked at Meeko and Flit. "Can you find a big branch? I need something John can lean on. Help me while I check John's injury."

Meeko and Flit searched the area. Finally Meeko dragged a long beechwood branch out from under a dead tree. At one end, the branch split into a fork, making a V-shape. John could put the branch under his arm and rest it in the V-shaped part.

"Oh, Meeko. It's a perfect crutch. Thanks," Pocahontas said. Meeko beamed.

John stood, holding on to the rock wall. Pocahontas gave him the crutch. "Here, this should help you walk. I'll support your other side."

Tired, cold, and injured, John and Pocahontas struggled up the path through the swirling snow.

CHAPTER 7

ocahontas feared that John would collapse. Her own ankle was swollen and painful. Her head and body ached. "I wish we were back in the village, safe in Father's house," she said.

At the thought of her father, her spirits lifted. If Nakoma had gone back to the village for help, then her father would have a search party out looking for them. They would be found soon.

The wind had died down, and it was

easier now to see the path before them.

"Come on, John. Can you walk a little faster? It's not blowing as hard, so we can make up some time. We're almost to the top." She urged him on.

John moved a little faster. But it didn't last long. His pace slowed and he started shaking. "So cold," he said through chattering teeth. And then he fell to the ground, dropping the crutch.

Pocahontas lightly slapped John's cheeks. "Come on, John. This is no time for sleep. Up we go."

Supporting him under one arm, she helped him up. Meeko brought the crutch. They continued upward.

Finally they reached the top of the cliff. Pocahontas stared at the snow-covered forest. She was so cold she couldn't feel her hands and feet. She knew that wasn't good. Her injured ankle was only a dull ache.

"Meeko, Flit, are you still with us?" She looked around, and the two animals came

to her. Meeko hopped onto Pocahontas's shoulder. He draped his body around her neck, covering her with his warm fur.

Pocahontas smiled. "Oh, my friend, thank you."

Meeko made room for Flit to sit on Pocahontas's shoulder. John leaned against Pocahontas, muttering.

After walking a while, they came to a clearing. Pocahontas stopped, expecting to see the edge of the cornfield outside her village.

But something was wrong. They had gone in the wrong direction. This was the Enchanted Glade, the home of Grandmother Willow!

John said in a faint voice, "I can't walk anymore. Pain's too great. I must sleep." He slipped to the ground and lay in the snow, near the river in the glade.

"Pocahontas. Is that you?" A smiling face appeared in the gnarled trunk of an old willow tree.

"Oh, Grandmother Willow, I don't think I can get us home."

"First of all, dear, stop crying," said Grandmother Willow.

Pocahontas wiped her eyes.

"You have great strength, Pocahontas, and John's spirit is with you."

"But I can't find my way in the snow."

"Listen to the spirits of the wind, the earth, the sky. They will guide you. Follow the river. Now go!"

Pocahontas helped John up. She propped his crutch under his arm. Holding him up on his other side, she turned and waved. "Thank you, Grandmother Willow. Good-bye."

They started through the forest along the river. Ice had begun to form along the edges. Pocahontas remembered Grandmother Willow's words and looked up at the sky. She could just make out the position of the sun through a lighter patch of clouds.

Pocahontas looked carefully at trees and bushes for clues to help her find her way. The moss on the tree trunks told her which way was north. Even with the snow, Pocahontas knew the forest well enough to recognize some landmarks.

Pocahontas put her face up to the wind in one direction and sniffed. Then she turned and smelled the faint odor of wood smoke in the wind. That would be from the fires of the village. She steered John that way through the blizzard.

Pocahontas struggled with all her might to keep them going. John was heavy, leaning on her with all his weight. The weather and their injuries seemed to be winning.

Just as they reached the edge of the cornfield outside the village, exhaustion overcame Pocahontas. She fell, letting go of John. Meeko and Flit spilled onto the ground. The last thing she heard was John calling, "Pocahontas, Pocahontas."

CHAPTER 8

"Pocahontas, Pocahontas." She heard her name being called. It must be John. She had to help him. Pocahontas opened her eyes.

She recognized the rush mats that covered the inside of her father's house. A cheery fire was burning in the shallow pit under the smoke hole. She saw the face of her father, looking at her with a mixture of love and concern.

"How do you feel?" he asked.

Pocahontas couldn't remember what had happened or how she had gotten here. She tried to think. She remembered falling off the cliff wall into the gorge. After that, it was confusing.

"How did I get here?" she asked.

"We found you in the cornfield. We've been out searching for you for hours. I was afraid we might not find you," her father said tenderly.

Pocahontas tried to move and felt a pain in her leg.

"Be careful," said her father. "Your leg is cut, and your ankle is sprained. You also have a slight head injury."

She stopped trying to move her aching body. "Where's John?" she asked.

Chief Powhatan looked confused. "John?"

"John Smith, Father. He's come back here. He was with me."

"No one was with you, daughter. You were alone, except for Meeko and Flit.

John Smith is still in England." Powhatan motioned to someone sitting on a mat in the shadows.

Nakoma came over to the mat where Pocahontas lay. "Hello, my friend. I'm glad to see you're awake. I've been so worried about you." Meeko, with Flit perched on his head, also came toward Pocahontas. Percy was watching attentively.

Pocahontas looked at Nakoma and her thoughts began to clear. "We were going to gather chinquapin nuts," she said. "And I fell."

Nakoma nodded. "I took Percy with me and went to get help after you fell. When your father and the search party got back to the gorge with me, we couldn't find you. We thought you might have been wandering, dazed because you hit your head. So we searched all around the gorge. Percy found your trail and tracked you until the snow got too heavy. Then we came back here and found you at the edge of the cornfield."

Nakoma looked amazed as she went on. "I don't know how you did it, but you got yourself back to the village, even with the snow and your injuries. Everyone in the village is talking about it."

"But I didn't get back alone. John was with me. He found me. He was helping me to get home. Then we ran into Ratcliffe in the woods with two awful men. He's here, Father!" Pocahontas sounded frightened.

Powhatan and Nakoma exchanged worried glances. "Tell us the rest of your story," Powhatan said.

Pocahontas told them about the fight with Ratcliffe and his men, how John had been injured and she had helped him.

When she finished, Powhatan said in a kind voice, "There have been no ships this week. John and Ratcliffe are not here, my child. I'm afraid everything you think happened was just a dream."

Pocahontas looked confused. "But it seemed so real, Father."

Nakoma held a branch out. "Was this the crutch?" she asked Pocahontas.

"Yes," Pocahontas said, excited.

"You were holding on to that branch when we found you. You wouldn't let it go," Powhatan said.

"Your ankle was wrapped with rush grass. And you had your belt around the cut on your leg, just the way you said you put it around John's cut. You must have wrapped your swollen ankle and bandaged your own leg," Nakoma told her.

"But what about Ratcliffe and the men? The fight?" she asked.

"Your fear made pictures of them in your dream." Powhatan knelt by Pocahontas and took her in his arms. "John is still real to you, Pocahontas. He is in there." He pointed to her heart. "John's spirit helped you keep up your strength and make your way home. Your thoughts

of John Smith saved your life." Powhatan stood up.

"Now I think Nakoma and I should let you get some rest. You need to heal."

Nakoma knelt beside Pocahontas. "Sleep well, my friend. " She rose and left with Powhatan.

Pocahontas lay on her mats, thinking about her ordeal. Even though she was disappointed that John Smith had not really come back, she took new comfort in their friendship. John's spirit would always be with her.

Flit left Meeko's head and flew down to Pocahontas's shoulder. Meeko and Percy crept over to Pocahontas and lay by her side. Pocahontas smiled. Then she fell asleep.